ABOYNE ACADEMY
LIBRARY

ABOYNE ACADEMY
LIBRARY

D0411066

Winnie the Witch

Three Story Treasury

Korky Paul and Valerie Thomas

The stories in this book are:

Winnie the Witch
Winnie in Winter
and
Winnie Flies Again

ABOYNE ACADEMY
LIBRARY

OXFORD
UNIVERSITY PRESS

Winnie the Witch

Winnie the Witch lived in a black
house in the forest.
The house was black on the outside
and black on the inside.
The carpets were black.
The chairs were black.
The bed was black and it had
black sheets and black blankets.
Even the bath was black.

Winnie lived in her black house
with her cat, Wilbur. He was black too.
And that is how the trouble began.

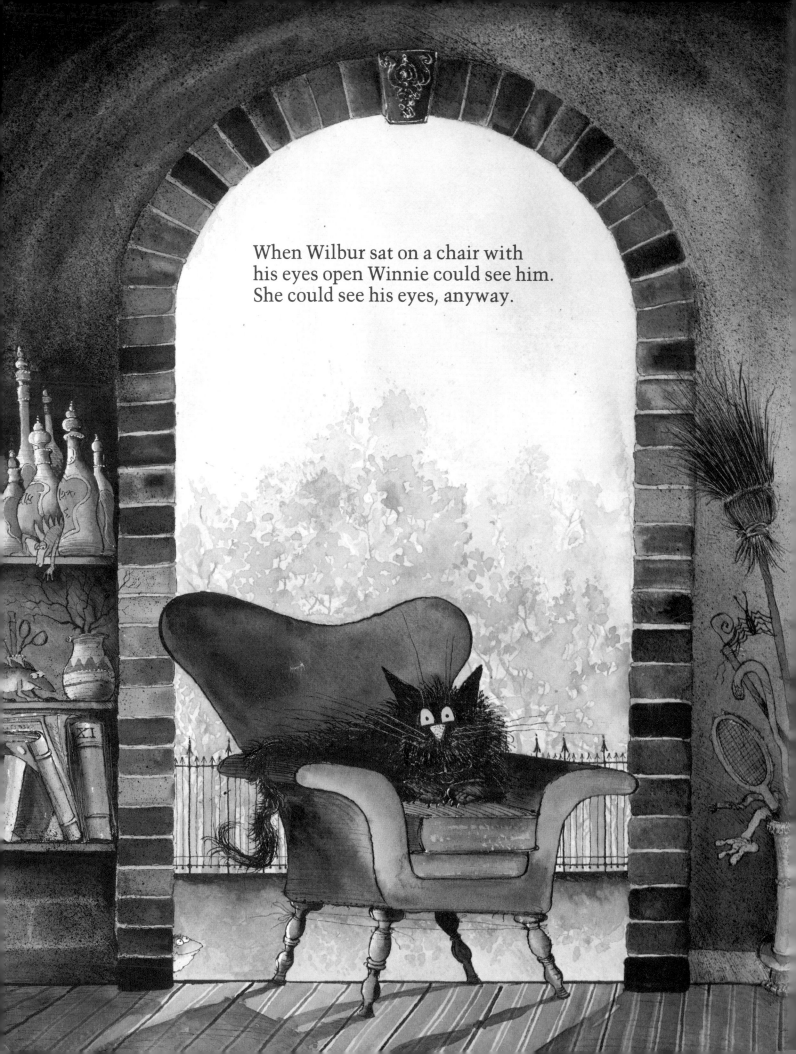

When Wilbur sat on a chair with
his eyes open Winnie could see him.
She could see his eyes, anyway.

But when Wilbur closed his eyes
and went to sleep,
Winnie couldn't see him at all.
So she sat on him.

When Wilbur sat on the carpet
with his eyes open, Winnie could see him.
She could see his eyes anyway.

But when Wilbur closed his eyes
and went to sleep,
Winnie couldn't see him at all.
So she tripped over him.

One day, after a nasty fall, Winnie
decided something had to be done.
She picked up her magic wand,
waved it once and ABRACADABRA!
Wilbur was a black cat no longer.
He was bright green!

Now, when Wilbur slept on a chair,
Winnie could see him.

When Wilbur slept on the floor,
Winnie could see him.

And she could see him when he slept on the bed.
But, Wilbur was not allowed to sleep on the bed . . .

. . . so Winnie put him outside.
Outside in the grass.

Winnie came hurrying outside,
tripped over Wilbur,
turned three somersaults,
and fell into a rose bush.

When Wilbur sat outside in the grass,
Winnie couldn't see him,
even when his eyes were wide open.

This time, Winnie was furious.
She picked up her magic wand,
waved it five times and . . .

. . . ABRACADABRA! Wilbur had a red head,
a yellow body, a pink tail, blue whiskers,
and four purple legs.
But his eyes were still green.

Now, Winnie could see Wilbur when
he sat on a chair, when he lay on the
carpet, when he crawled into the grass.

And even when he climbed to the
top of the tallest tree.

Wilbur climbed to the top of the tallest tree to hide.
He looked ridiculous and he knew it.
Even the birds laughed at him.

Next morning Wilbur was
still up the tree.
Winnie was worried.
She loved Wilbur and hated
him to be miserable.

Wilbur was miserable.
He stayed at the top of the tree
all day and all night.

Then Winnie had an idea.
She waved her magic wand and
ABRACADABRA! Wilbur was a
black cat once more.
He came down from the tree, purring.

Then Winnie waved her wand again, and again, and again.

Now instead of a black house,
she had a yellow house with a
red roof and a red door.
The chairs were white with red
and white cushions. The carpet
was green with pink roses.

The bed was blue, with pink and
white sheets and pink blankets.
The bath was a gleaming white.

And now, Winnie can see Wilbur
no matter where he sits.

For my wife Suzie – KP

Winnie in Winter

Winnie the Witch looked out of her window and shivered.
Her garden was covered in snow.
Her pond was covered in ice.
Icicles hung from the roof tops.
'I'm tired of winter,' said Winnie.

Wilbur came in through the cat flap.
His feet were wet, and his whiskers
were frozen.
Wilbur was tired of winter, too.

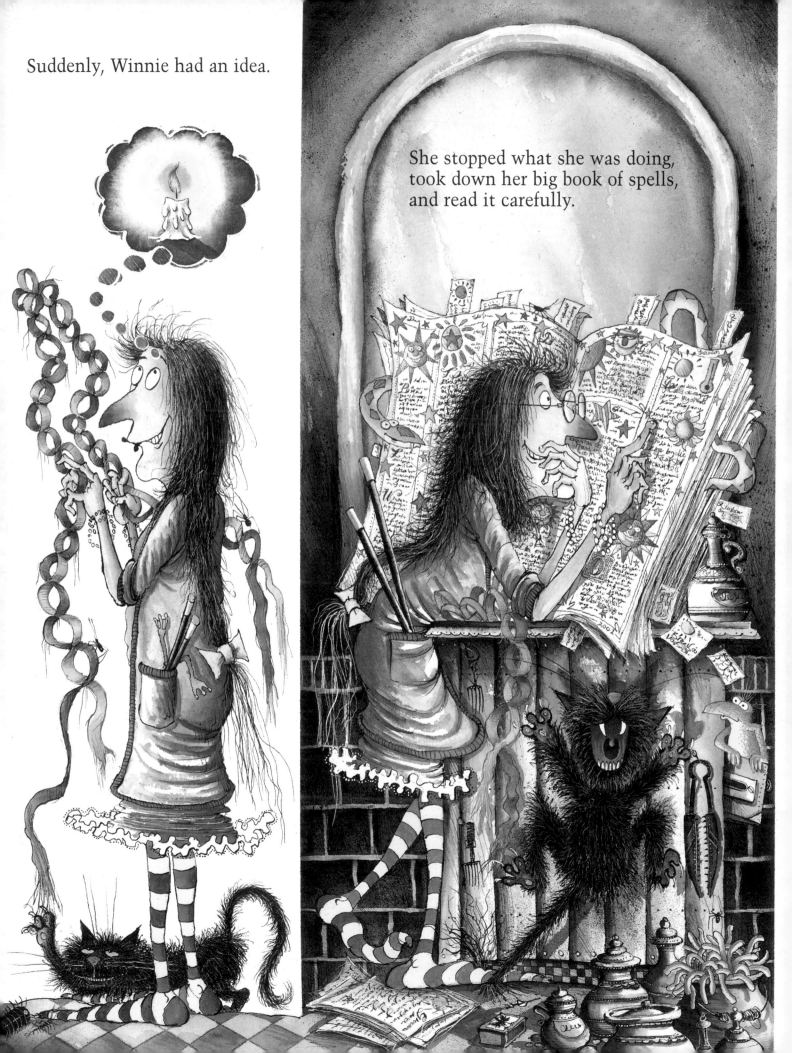

Suddenly, Winnie had an idea.

She stopped what she was doing, took down her big book of spells, and read it carefully.

Then she put on her woolly coat, her fluffy hat,
her snow boots, her gloves, and her scarf.
She picked up her wand and she went outside.

Wilbur already had a fur coat on, so he went
outside too. He thought something exciting
might happen, and he wanted to watch.

Winnie shut her eyes.
Then she stood on tiptoe, counted to ten,
waved her wand five times, and shouted,

ABRACADABRA!

And something magical happened!

Above Winnie's house the sun shone brightly.
The sky was deep blue.
All the snow had disappeared.
It was no longer winter at Winnie's house.
It was sunny summer.

Winnie took off her woolly coat, her fluffy hat,
her snow boots, her gloves, and her scarf.
She got her deck chair and went out in the
garden to sit in the sun.
'This is lovely,' said Winnie.
'Summer is much nicer.'

Wilbur lay down in the sun and purred.
This is lovely, he thought.
Summer is much nicer than winter.

All over the garden, little animals were waking up.
They had been having their winter sleep, and they
were very cross.

They came out into the garden, yawning sleepily.
'It's too early for summer,' they grumbled.
'We want to go back to sleep.'

The flowers had been asleep under the snow.
They woke up and began to grow.
Up came the leaves, and then the flowers.

But the sun was too hot for them.
Their heads began to droop.
All the lovely flowers were dying.

Winnie was worried.
The animals and the flowers didn't like
her lovely summer.

Then she heard a very strange noise . . .

Winnie turned around, and there behind her
was a great crowd of people.
They were running along the road towards her house.

They crowded into her garden.
They took off their coats, their hats,
their boots, their gloves,
and their scarves.

Then they sat in the sunshine.
They walked on Winnie's flowers.
They put orange peel on Winnie's grass.
They paddled in Winnie's pond.

Soon there was no room for Winnie
and Wilbur in the garden.
They went inside and looked out
of the window.
The noise was horrible.
The mess was horrible.
Winnie's lovely summer was horrible.

Then Winnie heard another strange noise.
A tinkling noise . . .

Somebody was selling ice creams in her garden.

Winnie was furious.
She grabbed her wand.
She rushed outside.
She stamped her foot, shut her eyes,
counted to ten, waved her wand five times
and shouted,

ABRACADABRA!

The sun disappeared.
The blue sky disappeared.
And the snow began to fall.

The people put on their coats, their hats, their boots,
their gloves, and their scarves, and rushed home.
The animals went back to bed, to finish their winter sleep.
The flowers went back under the ground to wait for spring.

Winnie and Wilbur went back inside.
Winnie made a cup of hot chocolate
and toasted a muffin.
Wilbur had a saucer of warm milk.

Then Winnie snuggled into bed.
Wilbur curled up at the foot of
the bed and purred.
'This is warm and cosy,' said Winnie.
'Winter is lovely too.'

For Sharon and Martin, who are always full of good ideas V.T.
For Ron Heapy K.P.

Winnie Flies Again

Winnie the Witch always travelled by broomstick.
It was a wonderful way to travel.

Winnie would jump onto her broomstick.
Wilbur would jump onto her shoulder.
And they would zoom up into the sky.

There were no traffic lights.
No traffic jams.

Just the empty sky.

Well, that was how it used to be.
But, just lately, the sky had become
rather crowded.

Last week, Winnie didn't see a helicopter.
Wilbur lost two of his whiskers.

The week before that, she didn't
see a hang glider.

Wilbur's tail was bent.

The week before that, a very tall building suddenly got in her way.

Wilbur lost a clump of fur.

'The sky is too dangerous, Wilbur,' said Winnie.
'We'll have to try something else.'
So she took out her wand, waved it, and shouted

ABRACADABRA!

Her broomstick turned into a bicycle.
But it was very slow.
Very hard to pedal.

And then a pond got in Winnie's way.
'She should look where she's going,' croaked a frog.

'A bicycle is worse than a broomstick, Wilbur,' said Winnie.
'We'll have to try something else.'
So she took out her wand, waved it, and shouted

ABRACADABRA!

Her bicycle turned into a skateboard.
The skateboard was fast.
But it was hard to steer.
And impossible to stop.

Winnie was stopped. By an ice-cream seller.
'Can't you see where you're going?' he shouted.

'A skateboard is worse than a bicycle, Wilbur,' said Winnie.
'We'll have to try something else.'
So she took out her wand, waved it, and shouted

ABRACADABRA!

Her skateboard turned into a horse,
and they trotted slowly down the path.
'This is much better than bicycles or skateboards,'
said Winnie.

But she didn't see . . .

. . . the low branch of a tree.
This time, Winnie didn't say anything.
She was hanging from a branch.

Slowly and carefully, Winnie climbed down from the tree.

'I think we'll walk home, Wilbur,' said Winnie.

They limped slowly along the road.
It was a very very slow way to travel.

But it was safe.

Until Winnie stepped into a hole
and tumbled deep down under the ground.

YES
WE'RE
OPEN

'I think I need a cup of tea,'
Winnie said.

Winnie climbed out of the tunnel and went into a shop.

'A cup of tea and a muffin, please,' she said.
'And a saucer of milk for my cat.'

'We don't sell cups of tea or muffins,'
said the shop lady.
'And we don't have saucers of milk.
But I think I can help you.'

And she sold Winnie a pair of spectacles.

Now, Winnie and Wilbur travel everywhere by broomstick.
It's a wonderful way to travel.

OXFORD
UNIVERSITY PRESS

Great Clarendon Street, Oxford OX2 6DP

Oxford University Press is a department of the University of Oxford.
It furthers the University's objective of excellence in research, scholarship,
and education by publishing worldwide in

Oxford New York

Athens Auckland Bangkok Bogotá Buenos Aires
Cape Town Chennai Dar es Salaam Delhi Florence Hong Kong Istanbul
Karachi Kolkata Kuala Lumpur Madrid Melbourne Mexico City Mumbai
Nairobi Paris São Paulo Shanghai Taipei Tokyo Toronto Warsaw

with associated companies in Berlin Ibadan

Oxford is a registered trade mark of Oxford University Press
in the UK and in certain other countries

Copyright © Valerie Thomas 1987, 1996, 1999, 2001
Illustrations copyright © Korky Paul 1987, 1996, 1999, 2001
The moral rights of the author and artist have been asserted

Database right Oxford University Press (maker)

This book first published 2001
Winnie the Witch first published 1987
Winnie in Winter first published 1986
Winnie Flies Again first published 1999
The stories are complete and unabridged

All rights reserved. No part of this publication may be reproduced,
stored in a retrieval system, or transmitted, in any form or by any means,
without the prior permission in writing of Oxford University Press.
Within the UK, exceptions are allowed in respect of any fair
dealing for the purpose of research or private study, or criticism or
review, as permitted under the Copyright, Designs and Patents Act 1988,
or in the case of reprographic reproduction in accordance with
the terms of the licences issued by the Copyright Licensing Agency.
Enquiries concerning reproduction outside these terms and in other
countries should be sent to the Rights Department, Oxford University Press,
at the address above.

This book is sold subject to the condition that it shall not, by way of trade or
otherwise, be lent, re-sold, hired out, or otherwise circulated without the
publisher's prior consent in any form of binding or cover other than that in
which it is published and without a similar condition including this condition
being imposed on the subsequent purchaser.

British Library Cataloguing in Publication Data available

ISBN 0 19 279 084 6

3 5 7 9 10 8 6 4 2

Printed in Spain